Sophia 🐾
the BIONIC cat

KAROLYN SMITH

Traitmarker Books
2984 Del Rio Pike
Franklin, TN 37069

Ordering Information for Quantity Sales:
(Special discounts are available on quantity purchases by corporations, associations, and others. For details, contact the author at the address above)

ATTRIBUTIONS
Interior Text Font: Open Dyslexic
Title Font: OpenDyslexicAlt, Christopher Hand, Skriix
Illustrator: James Craig Busike
Cover Design: Robbie Grayson III

BOOK PUBLISHING INFORMATION
ISBN 978-1-68419-345-5
Published by Traitmarker Books
Franklin, Tennessee
traitmarkerbooks.com
traitmarker@gmail.com

Printed in the United States of America

DEDICATION

Thanks to my family and friends for their continued encouragement: especially the Warfighter community for their unwavering support.

A special thank you to Boone Cutler: a Warfighter, a Veteran's best advocate, and my dear friend who made this book possible.

Thanks to Operation Mend: a program that not only healed my broken body, but saved my soul. Without Dana Katz and her program filled with loving and dedicated workers, I wouldn't have been able to write this book.

When I was born, it was late May. The leaves had all fallen, and the sky was all gray. I tried to get up and walk that day, but I soon discovered that I wasn't born the same way.

You see, you have two hands and you have two feet. You have two eyes, and you have big teeth. Now I have two ears and I have small teeth. I have small claws and I'm missing some feet.

When you count to four, I only count to three. But nobody ever told me I needed more feet. How will I jump so high to the sink, and how will I run with only three feet?

I fell down once, and I fell down twice. And I fell down three times and I was a fright.

"Get up! Get up!" a voice came from the night. "Get up now, and it will be a delight!"

I wiggled and squirmed to take a stand, but with one missing paw I needed a hand.

As the voice moved closer to cheer
me along, I began to hear
my Victory Song.

"Sophia, Sophia, you don't need a paw. You were born to brave it all! Now lean on me as I show you the way, because today is Sophia's day!"

With three paws - not four - I had made my way, along with Leo, today was a good day. "Three paws up!" Leo would say. "Three paws up ALL THE WAY!"

As we walked and walked and stumbled along...

I began to wonder
where my mom had gone.

"Does she look like me?" I said aloud. "Or does she have to walk just like the crowd? Does she walk with a limp or will she stand tall? Can she face danger and sing to her own song?"

As I wondered who my mom might be,
I smacked right into Victory.

While this Soldier didn't quite look like me, she picked me up as tender as can be.

As I'm in her arms. she kissed me all over. She put me down and gave Leo a once over.

"Wait a minute, wait a minute - you don't look like me! You have two hands, and you have two feet!"

"Oh, silly Sophia," my new mom did say,
"Some things don't always have to look
the same way!"

As mom walked over with a box in her hand, I had no idea she would help me take my stand.

As I unwrapped the bow and peeked inside,
I fell down hard and started to cry...

"MOMMY! MOMMY! Do you see what I see?
Hey, Leo, guess what?
MOMMY GOT ME NEW FEET!"

"Don't be sad," Mom did say. "Some of us were just born to be brave!"

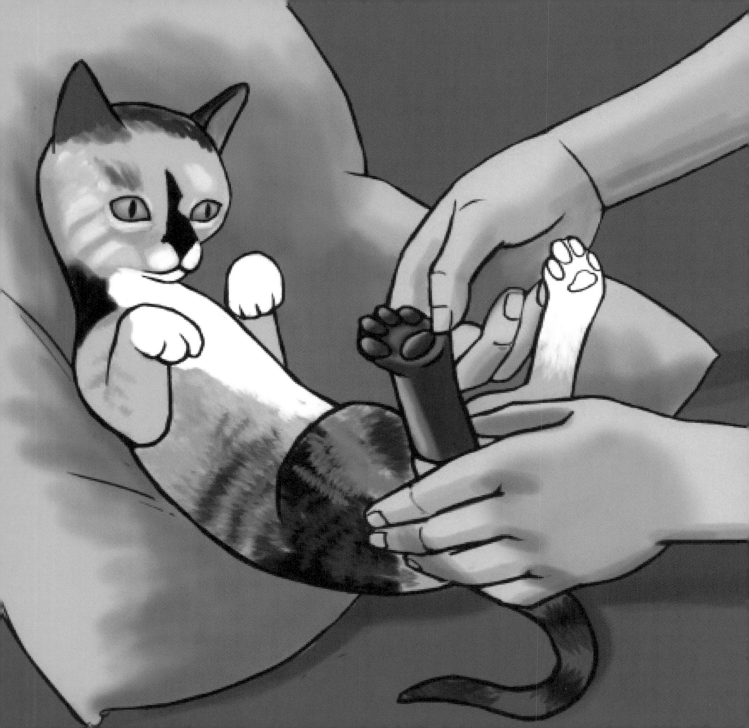

It was finally time to try on my new paw. I felt supersonic, bionic and all!

As she flopped on the floor and took a big pause, she didn't realize she just ran with FOUR paws!

Sophia stood up and shouted with glee,
"THREE PAWS UP is no longer me.
Today I stand in VICTORY!"

"I'm FOUR PAWS now as I sing my song, and we encourage you all to follow along!"

ABOUT THE ILLUSTRATOR

Jim Busike is a graduate of California College of the Arts with a BFA in Illustration. A professional artist since 1987, Jim currently teaches Game Development for the Art Institute Inland Empire campus. Jim's creative proficiencies include the field of character art with contributions to shipped titles like Final Four Basketball 99 – 04, JetX20, Darkwatch and The Bourne Conspiracy. Jim lives in San Diego with his wife and two daughters.

ABOUT THE AUTHOR

Karolyn Smith is a combat-wounded Veteran of Operation Iraqi Freedom (OIF2), author, and inspirational speaker. Karolyn's message of *Believe, Achieve and Succeed* has led her from the gritty streets of Baghdad, Iraq as a crew serve-machine gunner to the corporate offices of a financial firm providing high-threat security protection worldwide.

After years of struggling with injuries sustained and left untreated by Veteran Affairs (VA), Karolyn is recipient of the newest medical technology provided on behalf of Operation Mend at UCLA. The modus operandi of Karolyn's own recovery is the cornerstone of her passion for helping her Warfighter/Veteran community transition home and heal from the wounds of war.

Additionally, Karolyn aims to bring Sophia to the bedsides of children afflicted with some of the most serious illnesses in the country. Providing comfort and aid for others through selfless service has always been the focal point of her one-to-one mentoring and public speaking. You can learn about Karolyn and Sophia's story in more detail here:

http://www.people.com/article/amputee-cat-to-comfort-veterans

ABOUT OPERATION MEND
www.operationmend.ucla.edu

After years of severe and chronic pain, I was accepted into Operation Mend UCLA, a non-profit organization that provides combat-wounded Veterans, at no cost to the Veteran, the newest technology to heal their injuries. When the VA failed to help heal me, Operation Mend stepped in and provided a cutting-edge, multiple-layer, spinal fusion with a biomorphagenic technology discovered by UCLA.

***

To PURCHASE Sophia the Bionic Cat OR To REQUEST Karolyn Smith to speak to your organization or school, go to www.3pawsup.com

***

OTHER PLACES where you can find Karolyn and Sophia:

www.facebook.com/sophiathebioniccat

www.youtube.com/channel/UC0C_0PDQteQbtREZR1UOl_g

@SophiaBionicCat

CPSIA information can be obtained at www.ICGtesting.com
Printed in the USA
BVIW12n2143151216
470972BV00012B/53